Best Loved Stories

TREASURE ISLAND

by Robert Louis Stevenson

abridged edition

The Old Sea Dog

Squire Trelawney, Dr. Livesey and other friends have asked me to tell the story of our adventure on Treasure Island, so I take up my pen and go back to the time when my father kept the 'Admiral Benbow' inn, and the old brown seaman, with the sabre cut, first took up his lodging under our roof.

He was a tall, strong man, with a pigtail, like other sea-dogs. His clothes were ragged and his luggage consisted of a heavy sea-chest. He turned up singing the old sea-song I was to hear so often: "Fifteen men on a dead man's chest — yo-ho-ho, and a bottle of rum."

He inquired about the company at the inn, which was then nearly empty, glanced out at the bay and the cliffs surrounding it and said: "This is the berth for me. I'm a plain man: rum and bacon and eggs is what I want, and that cliff up there to watch the ships from. What are you to call me? Call me captain. Here's gold for you — and tell me when I've worked through it."

Bad as his clothes were, and coarsely as he spoke, he had the air of a man used to command, so it was no effort to address him as captain, although we never discovered what ship he had commanded. He was a very silent man, and spent his days hanging about the bay; while in the evening he sat in a corner of the parlour next to the fire, drinking rum.

Every day, when he came back from his stroll, he

would ask if any seafaring men had gone by along the road, and he told me to let him know at once if I ever saw a sailor with one leg.

There were nights when the captain took more rum that he could carry, and then he would sing his wicked old song, minding nobody. Often he would make the company join in the chorus, and they would do so to keep him quiet, because he was a fearsome man when drunk.

In other words, he was a real old sea-dog, and whether they were believed or not his terrible stories scared people as much as his language shocked them.

One person, though, refused to be scared or shocked, and this was our good Dr. Livesey.

The doctor had come one evening to see my poor father, who was seriously ill, and went into the parlour to smoke a pipe until his horse was ready. Suddenly the captain began his eternal song: "Fifteen men on a dead man's chest — yo-ho-ho, and a bottle of rum!"

Doctor Livesey was the only one who had never heard it before. He looked angrily at the singer, and went on talking to old Taylor about his rheumatics. The captain, meantime, had gradually brightened up at his own music, and at last banged his fist on the table in a way that meant: silence. It was the signal for one of his horrible stories to begin.

All voices stopped, except Dr. Livesey's; he went on as before, speaking clearly and kindly. The cap-

tain banged on the table again, and, with an oath, cried: "Silence there, between decks!"

"Were you addressing me, sir?" said the doctor. And when he was told, with another oath, that this was so, he answered calmly: "I have only one thing to say to you, sir. If you keep on drinking rum, the world will soon be rid of a very dirty scoundrel!"

The old fellow's fury was awful. He sprang to his feet, drew and opened a sailor's clasp-knife, and threatened to pin the doctor to the wall. The doctor never moved, but spoke in the same tone of voice as before, calm and steady: "If you do not put that knife away this instant, you shall hang at the next assizes!" And he looked so firmly at him that the captain put away his weapon.

"I'm not a doctor only, I'm a magistrate," Dr. Livesey went on. "And if I hear any complaints against you I'll have you routed out of this place!" Soon afterwards he left, but the captain was quiet that evening, and bothered no one for many evenings ahead.

One morning the captain had risen earlier than usual, and set out down the beach. My mother was upstairs, seeing to my father, and I was laying the table for the captain's breakfast, when the door opened and a repulsive-looking stranger came in. He was not a sailor, and he had both his legs, yet the sight of him terrified me.

He asked for a glass of rum and while I was serving it said he had come to see his old friend Bill. It appeared that Bill was the captain.

I told him his friend had gone out, but would not be long away. At that very moment the stranger saw the captain returning, and grabbed my shoulder and dragged me into a corner behind the open door, telling me he was going to give his friend a surprise.

The Black Spot

Paralysed with fear, I stood, silent and still, waiting for whatever was to happen. The captain came in and marched straight across the room.

"Bill!" called the stranger, and the captain spun round and faced us.

"Black Dog!" he murmured, pale in the face.

"And who else?" said the stranger. Then he turned to me: "Now lad, leave us alone. I've got very private things to say to my friend!"

I left the room and for a while, though I did my best to listen, I could understand nothing of the talk, because they were speaking softly; but gradually their voices grew louder and I managed to catch a sentence or two of the captain's, though it made little sense.

"No, no, no! A thousand times no!" he cried once, and then, "We'll all be hanged!"

Suddenly there was a tremendous explosion of oaths and other noises — chairs overturned and the clash of steel. A cry of pain filled the house and the next moment I saw Black Dog in flight, followed by the captain, both with drawn cutlasses, and Black Dog wounded in the left shoulder. At the door, the captain aimed another terrific blow at the fugitive, one that would certainly have split him in two had our big signboard of Admiral Benbow not intercepted it.

Once out on the road, Black Dog took to his heels, and vanished in a moment. The captain staggered back into the house. I saw him steady himself against the wall and heard his voice whisper to me: "Jim, bring me some rum, I must get away from here."

I ran to fetch the rum, and as I was doing so I heard a heavy thud in the parlour. I rushed in and found the captain lying on the floor. Meantime my mother, alarmed at the sound of the fighting, had come down to see what had happened. We raised the captain's head; he was breathing hard.

We had no idea what to do to help the captain, so it was a relief when Dr. Livesey appeared, on his daily visit to my father.

"Oh, doctor," we cried. "What shall we do? Where is he wounded?"

"Wounded? He's no more wounded than you or I. He's had a stroke, as I warned him. Now, Mrs Hawkins, you run upstairs, while I do my best to save the wretch's life."

He bled the captain, and soon afterwards the sick man opened his eyes. When he first saw the doctor he frowned, but then he saw me, and looked relieved. Suddenly, though, he changed colour and asked anxiously: "Black Dog . . . where is he?"

"There's no Black Dog, except in your imagination," said the doctor. "You've drunk too much rum and what I warned you about has happened."

Then the doctor and I took the captain to his room and put him to bed.

About midday I went up to the captain with cool drinks. He was not much better, but his voice was stronger. "Jim," he said, "you're the only one here that's worth anything, and I've always been good to you. Tell me the truth now; how much longer must I stay in bed, according to that doctor?"

As there seemed no reason not to, I told him.

"A week? I can't do that! They'd have the black spot on me by then. If I should fall asleep and they tip me the black spot, it's my old sea-chest they're after. Run to that doctor fellow and tell him to come at once if he wants to lay hands on what's left of old Flint's crew, man and boy. I was old Flint's first mate, and I'm the only one that knows the place. Flint told me as he lay dying, d'you hear? But unless they get the black spot on me you mustn't tell; or unless you see Black Dog again, or the sea-faring man with one leg. Understand, Jim?"

"But what is the black spot, captain?" I asked.

"It's a summons, lad. I'll tell you if I get that. But keep your eyes open, and I'll go shares with you, on my honour!"

He rambled on a little longer, then he fell into a heavy sleep, and I left him. My poor father died quite suddenly that evening, and in my grief I forgot everything else. In the days that followed I was so busy that the captain's words went out of my mind; meantime the old fellow had got up and was dragging himself about, and in spite of his weakness managing to get through large quantities of rum.

A few days passed, and about three o'clock on a cold, foggy afternoon, when I was standing at the inn door, I saw a man approaching slowly. He was plainly blind, for he tapped before him with a stick, and in all my life I had never seen a more dreadful looking figure.

Outside the inn he stopped and, staring into space, said in a sing-song voice: "Will any kind friend tell a poor blind man where he is now?"

"You are at the Admiral Benbow, Black Hill Cove," I said.

"My kind young friend, will you lead me in?" he said, and held out his hand. Overcoming revulsion I took it, and the old man's fingers gripped mine like a vice. Frightened, I struggled to get away, but the blind man pulled me up to him.

"Now, boy," he said, "take me to the captain. And no tricks, mind!"

His cold, cruel voice cowed me more than his grip on my hand. I went indoors and towards the parlour.

"When you see him," said the old man, "call loudly: 'Here's a friend for you, Bill'. If you don't, I'll do this," and he gave me a terrible twitch.

Terrified, I opened the door and shouted the sentence. The captain looked up and in a moment he was sober, staring at us and trying to rise, but unable to do so.

"Bill," said the blind man, "stay where you are. I can't see, but I can hear a finger stirring! Boy, take his left hand by the wrist, and bring it to my right."

I did what he told me and saw something pass from the blind man's hand to the captain's. The old man at once let go of me and, with incredible speed and nimbleness, crossed the parlour and was out in the road. I stood still, listening to his stick tap-tapping into the distance. It was some moments before the captain or I gathered our wits again. Then I dropped his hand and he opened it and looked anxiously into the palm.

"Ten o'clock!" he cried. "Six hours ahead!"

He sprang up and, putting his hand to his throat, gave a kind of rattling sound; then he crashed to the floor, face downwards. The captain was dead.

Beside his hand was a small paper disc, black on one side, the fearsome black spot. On the white side was written: "You have till ten tonight". I then remembered the captain's words and told my mother everything. She guessed that if someone was after his sea-chest it was because there was something valuable in it, and declared that she would not let anyone take it until the dead man's debt had been paid.

We decided to examine the contents of the sea-chest. It was like any other on the outside, the initial "B" burned on the top and the corners smashed and broken by long, rough usage.

A strong smell of tobacco and tar rose from the inside, but nothing was to be seen except a suit of good clothes. Under that we found a quadrant, a pannikin, several sticks of tobacco, two brace of handsome pistols, an old Spanish watch, and a pair of compasses. At the very bottom we found a bundle of what looked like papers, tied in oilcloth, and a canvas bag in which coins jingled.

"I'll show these rogues I'm an honest woman," said my mother. "I'll have my dues, and not a farthing over." And she began to count the amount the captain owed her from the sailor's bag.

It was a long, difficult business, for the coins were

of all countries and sizes, all mixed up together, and my mother could really reckon only with the guineas, which were scarcer than the rest. When we were about halfway through, I suddenly put my hand on her arm, for I heard in the silent, frosty air, a sound that brought my heart into my mouth — the tap-tapping of the blind man's stick upon the road. It drew nearer and nearer, while we sat holding our breath. Then it struck sharp on the locked inn door, and we could hear the handle being turned, and the bolt rattling as the wretch tried to enter; and then there was a long silence. At last, to our indescribable relief, the tapping started up again.

I was sure he would soon be back with his friends, and I begged my mother to take refuge in the village.

But my mother wanted to take the money that was owed to us and told me she would not move until she had it. Suddenly, though, we heard a shrill whistle in the distance; then she too became frightened and decided to be content with the money she had already.

"And I'll take this to square things up," I said, picking up the oilskin packet. A moment later we were outside the inn.

We had gone only a few steps when we saw people coming towards us.

I looked round for a means of escape, and saw a small bridge across a ditch. Under it I dragged my mother, and, as it was too small a hiding place for us both, I ran and hid in a gorse bush. Only just in time, too! Soon afterwards seven or eight men came up. Three of them were together, the one in the middle the blind beggar.

They all went into the inn, and I heard shouts of rage: they had stumbled over the captain's body. Then I heard the blind man shouting orders. "Don't waste time! We've got to find Flint's packet, what ever happens!"

The search yielded nothing and I heard them cursing. Then the blind man and called to his companions to track us down at once — we could hardly be far. Just at that moment whistles were heard in the distance, and one of the scoundrels exclaimed: "It's Dick, warning us of danger. They must have thought we were smugglers and set the customs men on us. Hurry, let's get away!"

"Get away?" roared the blind beggar. "You fools, if we find Flint's packet it's riches! Look for the pair of them, hurry!"

The sound of galloping horses put an end to the quarrel. The men took to their heels in all directions, except for the blind beggar, who staggered about the road, begging the others not to abandon him.

Some customs men on horse-back rode up at that very moment, and the blind man, to escape what now seemed certain capture, started dashing away, but he tripped and was run down and dragged along by a galloping horse. A scream echoed through the darkness and the blind beggar rolled to the side of the road, never to rise again.

While the customs men were scattered about the countryside trying to catch what they thought were smugglers, I went to help my mother. She had fainted, but was soon herself again, and with one of the customs men I helped her to the village. The head of the customs men then let me mount behind him and ride over to Dr. Livesey's, to give him a report on what had occurred that evening at the Admiral Benbow.

Captain Flint's Man

We found Dr. Livesey at the Hall, where he was spending the evening with Squire Trelawney; I told them the whole story.

When I had finished I produced the oilskin packet and said I was sure it must have been what the blind beggar was looking for: Captain Flint's packet.

"Flint?" said the doctor. "Flint's the name of a notorious pirate who died some time ago. If those ruffians were looking for something that belonged to him, it must have something to do with the fabulous wealth Flint accumulated. If I'm right, and in this packet we find some clue to where Flint hid his treasure, would you, squire, be prepared to foot the bill for whatever it costs to allow Jim to get the treasure which by rights is his?"

"If we have the clue you talk about, I'll fit out a ship and take Jim to the ends of the earth, if Flint's treasure is there!"

"Very well, if Jim agrees, we'll open the packet," he said, and when I nodded he started unstitching it. Inside the oilskin were an exercise book and a map.

We opened the exercise book and found it full of strange entries and figures, a record of twenty years of piracy in which the captain had taken part, with the gains he had made during that time.

When we had looked at it and found nothing else, we turned to the map. It showed an island, with latitude and longitude, soundings, names of hills, bays and inlets, and details for a safe anchorage.

Three red crosses were marked on it, two on the north part of the island, and one in the south west, and beside this last, in a small neat hand very different from the captain's, was written: "*Bulk of treasure here*". On the back of the map the same hand had written this further information: "*Tall tree, spy-glass shoulder, bearing a point of the N. of NNE. — Skeleton Island ESE and by E. — Ten feet. — The bar silver is in the north cache; you can find it in the trend of the east hummock, ten fathoms south of the black crag. — The arms are in the sand hill, N. point of north inlet cape, bearing E. and a quarter N.J.F.*"

That was all. But brief as it was, and to me incomprehensible, it filled the squire and Dr. Livesey with delight. Indeed, the squire started making plans at once. "Tomorrow I'm off to Bristol and in a few days we'll have the best ship and crew in England. Hawkins shall be a splendid cabin-boy. You, Livesey, will be ship's doctor, and I the admiral. We'll take my gamekeeper Redruth and my servants Joyce and Hunter."

"No objections," said the doctor. "But we must all take care to be silent. We're not the only ones who know of this paper. The scoundrels who attacked the inn tonight will do anything to get Flint's map. You, sir, must hold your tongue, especially in Bristol."

"Livesey, you're right," said the squire. "I'll be as silent as the grave."

It was decided that I should stay with the doctor while the squire set off for Bristol to hire a ship and fit it for a long voyage. Squire Trelawney had the inn restored to my mother, and found a boy to take my place while I was treasure-hunting.

After a few days the squire wrote to say he had bought a fine ship and fitted her up. We must hurry to Bristol, where the *Hispaniola* was ready to set sail. This was encouraging news, but with it came further information which worried us.

It appeared that the squire had been talking, and now everyone in Bristol knew why the *Hispaniola* was sailing. He had also picked his crew in the most haphazard way: instead of trusting to Smollett, the ship's captain, to choose one, he had gone to John Silver, an old sailor who had lost a leg serving under Hawke, and was now landlord of a public house.

John Silver's misfortunes had touched Squire Trelawney, who had asked him to serve as ship's cook. We also learned that the crew consisted of about twenty, "of the toughest old salts — not pretty to look at, but of the most indomitable spirit."

All we could do was put a good face on it and pack our baggage. I slept for the whole journey, and woke when the coach stopped outside a large inn near Bristol, where Squire Trelawney, dressed as a naval officer, was waiting. He greeted us with: "Welcome to Bristol, my friends. We sail tomorrow!"

Next day Squire Trelawney gave me a note to take to John Silver, gaving him his sailing orders.

It was not hard to find the tavern, a bright little place with a street on either side, and an open door on both. I recognised the landlord, a tall strong man with his left leg cut off at the hip and a crutch under the shoulder.

I must confess that when we had first had the squire's letter I had been afraid John Silver might be the one-legged sailor so greatly feared by the captain, but a glance was enough to reassure me. I had seen the captain, and Black Dog, and the blind beggar, and I thought I knew what a buccaneer was like. John Silver, with his pleasant, merry air, could hardly be one. So, without the smallest hesitation, I went up to him and said: "Mr. Silver, sir? I have a note for you."

He looked at the note, then smiled at me in a friendly way. "I see!" he exclaimed. "You're our new cabin-boy, the grand fellow who turned the tables on a gang of scoundrels. I'm very happy to know you."

He had spoken quite loudly and several of the customers had turned to stare at me; but one of them suddenly rose and in a moment was out of the door. It was Black Dog.

"Oh," I cried, "stop him! It's Black Dog! One of the gang!"

"So? Ben, Harry, run and catch him!" said Silver. "That Black Dog — I've seen him before. He used to come with a blind man, Pew."

"I knew the blind beggar! He's one of the gang!"

"The scoundrels! Well, I've sent two good runners after him, and you'll see, he won't get away!"

When Ben and Harry returned saying they had not managed to catch up with him, Silver was furiously angry, and roared at them for a long time. When he quietened down he said he must go and say goodbye to his wife, and went into a room behind the parlour.

In a few minutes he was back, and made me a sign to follow him.

As we walked to the ship, my companion never stopped talking. He knew all the ships we passed and told me all kinds of things about them, and by the time we reached the *Hispaniola* I was convinced I had made a friend in John Silver.

As soon as we were on board Silver presented himself to the squire and the doctor, and told them what had happened, stopping occasionally to ask me to confirm this or that detail. At the end the two gentlemen congratulated him on what he had done and Silver replied that it was only his duty. He left us and Dr. Livesey told the squire: "Well, I will say this — John Silver suits me. I feel we'll always be able to trust him."

The squire was delighted, but his expressions of delight were cut short by the arrival of Captain Smollett, who asked to speak to him.

"Well sir," said the captain, after he had shut the door carefully behind him. "Better speak plain, I believe. I don't like this voyage, I don't like the men, and I don't like my officer, Arrow. I'll tell you why. I don't like the voyage because everyone knows we're going after treasure, and the crew's been chosen without my being consulted. Who can be sure they'll obey orders? We're taking powder and arms: wouldn't it be better to put them under the cabin, instead of in the fore-hold? Then sir, as you've got three of your own servants with you, why not give them berths here beside the cabin and the arms, instead of with the crew?"

"I see you fear a mutiny," said the doctor.

"Sir," said Captain Smollett, "I said no such thing. All our men may be excellent fellows, but I know nothing about them, and I'm responsible for the ship's safety and the life of every man on her. I have

a feeling things aren't going quite right, and I ask you to take certain precautions."

"Do as you like," said the squire with a gesture of annoyance, and the captain took his leave.

A few hours later, when the tide was right, Captain Smollett gave orders to sail. I went to the galley where John Silver, nicknamed Barbecue, broke into the song I knew all too well: "Fifteen men on a dead man's chest — Yo-ho-ho, and a bottle of rum!"

The crew joined in the chorus and the *Hispaniola* set sail, while I thought of my mother, and the Admiral Benbow, and all the things I loved and was leaving behind me. The crew's song had already given a certain sinister air to our departure, and this, together with my memories, excited me.

What I Found in the Apple Barrel

I am not going to tell of the voyage in any detail. It went well, for the ship was good, the crew capable, and the captain understood his business. All the same, before we reached Treasure Island, two or three things happened which I must mention.

First of all, Mr. Arrow turned out even worse than the captain had feared. Several times he was drunk, and one dark, stormy night he vanished overboard and no one was surprised, for this is the kind of thing that happens to drunkards at sea. Arrow's place was taken by Job Anderson, a friend of John Silver's.

The crew had a great admiration of John Silver

and he was friendly with them all. With me he was always kind, and always glad to see me in the galley, which he kept as clean as a new pin. Just as clean was the corner where his parrot's cage hung. The bird was called Captain Flint, because, according to Silver, she behaved like a pirate and had the language of a buccaneer.

When anyone came into the galley, the parrot would shriek: "Pieces of eight! Pieces of eight!"

On the evening before we should have sighted Treasure Island, the squire had a barrel of apples put on deck for the men, and when my work was over I thought I should like one.

The barrel was almost empty, so I climbed right inside it, and sitting down there to eat my apple, I must have fallen asleep, when someone suddenly leant against the barrel. I was about to jump up when the man began to speak and I recognised John Silver's voice. After the first few words, I would not have shown myself for all the world, but lay there, trembling and listening, for I had understood that the lives of all the honest men aboard depended on me alone.

"Of course," said Silver, "Flint was captain and I was quartermaster, but even Flint was afraid of me, and so were the rest of the crew, because I was cleverer than they were. What's become of Flint, and Bill, and Pew the blind man and all the others? Dead and gone, or else living like beggars. Whereas I've got some money put away and when I get home from this voyage I'll put the past behind me and live like a lord."

"But you won't dare show your face in Bristol after this," said Israel Hands, a wily old sailor.

"When we weighed anchor," said Silver, "my old missis sold the tavern, and went away. Now, listen to me, all of you. I know you're impatient to get going, but I don't know where Flint's map is, or who's got it. So I mean the squire and the doctor to find the stuff and help us to get it aboard. Then we'll see. We can put them ashore, or else kill them. What d'you say?"

"Dead men don't bite," said Israel. "Kill them."

"Right you are," said Silver.

Israel and Silver then talked softly together. I could catch very little of what they were saying, but I clearly heard this whole sentence: "Not another man of them will join." So there were still some faithful men left on board.

Just then a sort of brightness fell upon me in the barrel, and looking up I found the moon had risen. Almost at the same moment the voice of the lookout suddenly shouted: "Land ho!"

We Reach Treasure Island

I heard a great rush of feet across the deck and people tumbling up from the cabin. In a moment I had slipped out of my hiding place and, still trembling with fear, I went up to the doctor and murmured into his ear: "I have terrible news for you, sir. I must talk to you and Captain Smollett and the squire as soon as possible. Please meet me in the cabin."

A few minutes later the three of them were facing me in the cabin. I told them all I had heard, and nobody breathed while I was speaking. At the end the squire exclaimed: "Captain, you were right. I've been an ass and await your orders. What are you going to do to prevent these ruffians from carrying out their plan?"

"First of all we must avoid behaving in any way that might arouse their suspicions: in other words, we must behave perfectly naturally. If I gave orders to go about, they would mutiny at once. Very likely things will go smoothly till the treasure's found. In the meantime we must discover which of the men are faithful. For the moment we can count only on ourselves and the squire's three servants."

"Counting Hawkins," said the doctor, "that makes seven."

"Yes, six men and a boy," said the captain. "Whereas there are nineteen of them. We must keep our eyes open. Now let's get some sleep, and tomorrow we'll see what happens."

Next morning when I came on deck the island was about half a mile away. It was dominated by the strangely shaped Spy-glass hill.

A place to anchor was found and the captain asked if anyone had been on the island before and

could pilot the ship in. Silver came forward and said he had once been there, and remembered it perfectly. He said he would take the ship to a safe anchorage, not far from a kind of abandoned fortress, which could be used as a base for our operations on land.

Several boats were launched to tow the *Hispaniola* to the right point, a landlocked bay surrounded by thick woods. During the operation we had noticed signs of rebelliousness in the crew. We were not the only ones to have noticed the danger, though. Silver murmured warnings to his men and, by singing one song after another, did his best to hide their ill-temper. But how long would he be able to control the crew?

Captain Smollett held a council of war in the

cabin. "Silver's as anxious as we are to calm the men," he said. "He doesn't want them rising against us yet. Let's give him a chance to talk quietly to them, by sending the whole crew ashore for the afternoon. Silver'll bring them aboard again as mild as lambs."

It was so decided, and Captain Smollett went on deck to speak to the crew. "My lads, we've all had a hard trip, and a turn ashore won't hurt anyone. Take the boats and enjoy yourselves. Half an hour before sunset I'll fire a gun."

The silly fellows seemed to think they would stumble over the treasure the moment they landed, for they gave a loud cheer, then rushed for the boats. Not all of them, though. At a sign from Silver, six of the men stayed on board. With a sudden flash of inspiration, I decided to go ashore with the crew. I slipped into one of the boats, and it was only when we were near the beach that Silver noticed my presence. But I managed to leap ashore and dash into the nearest thicket.

"Jim, Jim!" Silver shouted after me, but I took no notice and ran on into a wood, where I hid.

Two men soon approached: Silver talking and a sailor, Tom, listening. I heard Silver say: "Tom, it's for your own good. You can't save yourself, because some of them have got it in for you . . ."

"Silver," said the man, his voice trembling with anger and indignation, "I'm going to do my duty and . . ."

A sudden noise interrupted him. I had found one of the honest men, and, at that very moment, I heard another. A cry of anger in the distance was immediately followed by a long, horrible scream, the cry of a man mortally wounded. Tom leaped at the sound, but Silver gave an evil smile.

"In God's name, John, what's up?" cried Tom.

"Oh, that'll be Alan. He had doubts, like you . . ."

"Alan! You've killed him, haven't you? Kill me, too, but I'll stick to my duty!"

And the brave young fellow turned his back on Silver and started walking back to the ship. He did not get far, though. With a shout, Silver grabbed his crutch and sent it hurtling through the air, point first, at Tom. It hit him violently in the back and he fell, half dead. Silver was on him in a moment and buried his knife in his defenceless body.

I began to crawl back as fast and as quietly as possible. I could hear Silver and the men shouting across the thicket, and as soon as I was clear of it I ran as I had never run before, hardly caring where I was going, so long as it took me away from the murderers.

Could anyone be in a worse position than I was? I could not get back to the *Hispaniola*, for as soon as they saw me among the boats, they would wring my neck like a snipe's. The fact that I had been on my own would prove that I had dangerous knowledge, and they could not let me get away with it.

It was all over. Goodbye to the *Hispaniola*, the

squire, the doctor and the captain! My fate was to die of hunger, or at the hands of the mutineers.

All this time, I was still running and without realising it I had drawn near to the foot of a little hill with two peaks.

And here a fresh alarm brought me to a standstill with a thumping heart. Some gravel, dislodged from the steep cliff-side, fell through the trees, and I looked in the direction of the sound. There I saw a shadow and stopped still, paralysed with fear.

Enter Ben Gunn

Was it man or beast? I could not tell. It was something dark and hairy — bear or monkey, even a man. The shadow seemed to be trying to head me off. I was tired, but even under the best conditions I should have been unable to race against such an adversary, who ran like a deer.

I suddenly remembered that I had a loaded pistol in my belt. Realising I was not defenceless gave me the courage to face the man and I walked up to him; to my great surprise, he flung himself on his knees and held his hands out imploringly.

"Have pity," he cried in English, in a hoarse, hesitant voice. "Have pity on a poor man who hasn't spoken to anyone these three years."

"Were you shipwrecked? Who are you?"

"Ben Gunn, and I wasn't shipwrecked. I was marooned."

I shuddered, knowing this was a terrible punishment inflicted by buccaneers on those who disobeyed the rules of piracy. So Ben Gunn was an outlaw! He seemed to read my thoughts, and continued in pleading tones: "Don't be afraid of me. I'm honest and I'm rich. Rich, I tell you! Rich! Rich! What's your name? Jim? Well, Jim, you haven't come in Flint's ship, have you?"

I told him what had brought us, and how John Silver and his friends were involved.

"John Silver, did you say? I know him, know him well. This is an ugly business, but Ben Gunn'll help. Will your squire prove generous and give me, say, a thousand pounds out of the money that's as good as his? And take me back with him?"

I reassured him and, he told me his story. As a youngster, he had been on Flint's ship and seen the treasure taken ashore. Years later, on another pirate ship, he had sailed near the island and persuaded some of the others to jump ship and go treasure hunting with him. After twelve days of searching and finding nothing, they left him on the island with a musket, a spade and a pickaxe. Three years had gone.

"Tell my story to your squire, Jim," he said.

"Right," I said. "But I can't get back to the ship."

"Why, there's my boat, hidden by the white rock."

At that moment a cannon thundered out.

"They've begun to fight!" I cried. "Follow me!"

After a time the cannonshot was followed by small-arms fire, and I could not understand what was happening. I was surprised to see the Union Jack fluttering above the trees ahead of me. What had happened?

Dr. Livesey told me later. When he realised that I had landed, and that it was impossible to take over the ship, he, the squire and the captain agreed that he should go ashore to protect me.

He and Hunter took a boat and landed a short way from where the crew had done so. He left Hunter in charge of the boat and went into the thicket. After less than a hundred yards he came to a clearing, in the middle of which stood the old pirates' stockade.

This was how it was: a spring of clear water rose almost at the top of a knoll. On this knoll, and covering the spring, they had built a stout log-house, which at a pinch could have held forty people, and was holed for musketry on every side. All round this they had cleared a wide space, and around the space put a fence about six feet high, without door or opening, too strong to pull down quickly or easily, and too open to shelter anyone attacking from out-side. The people in the log-house would have the advantage in every way. They could stay quietly inside and pick off their attackers like partridges. All they wanted was good watch and food, and they could hold out against a regiment.

Dr. Livesey, who had served in the army, realised

all this at a glance, and what particularly took his fancy was the spring. The cabin of the *Hispaniola* was a good enough shelter, with plenty of arms, ammunition and food, but it had no water.

While he was looking at the stockade, he heard Alan's scream, and thought that I was the victim. He ran back to the boat, Hunter rowed him fast to the ship, and there he told his anxious friends the plans he had been making. Old Redruth was put on guard at the cabin door, with orders to stop the crew from getting astern; then Hunter brought the boat round and he and Joyce started loading her up with weapons, ammunition and food. The squire and the captain, with pistols, forced the six men Silver had left on board to do nothing to stop them.

When the boat was full, Dr. Livesey, Hunter and Joyce took everything ashore, and carried it to the stockade. Joyce and Hunter stayed guarding the stores, while the doctor went back to the ship and loaded the boat a second time. What would not go into it they flung overboard. Unfortunately they forgot the cannon, and, as we shall see, this lapse proved nearly fatal to them.

The captain, before leaving the *Hispaniola*, had an idea. "Now, men," he called, "do you hear me? I am leaving this ship, and I order you to follow your captain. I give you thirty seconds to join me."

There was a sudden scuffle, a sound of blows, and out burst Abraham Gray with a knife-cut on his cheek. He came running to the captain, calling: "I'm with you, sir, even if it costs me my life!"

Next minute he and the captain had dropped into the boat, but it was overloaded and could move only very slowly.

The ebb tide was now running, and adding to their troubles; a strong rippling current was carrying the small boat off course and out to sea.

"We must hope the current slackens, and we can get ashore," said the captain; and then suddenly, he exclaimed: "The cannon! Look astern, doctor!"

My Friends Abandon Ship

Dr. Livesey looked round; the five men aboard were taking the cover off the cannon. "They may not hit us. Firing that isn't the same as using a rifle."

"Israel Hands was Flint's gunner," said Gray.

"Then we'd better do something at once," said Captain Smollett. "Mr. Trelawney, will you pick off one of those men, sir? Hands, if possible."

The squire raised his gun and fired. But at the very moment he did so Hands stooped down, and the ball hit one of the others. His cry was echoed not only by his companions on board but by the other pirates, who had just come out of the trees and were tumbling into their boats.

"Row fast, even if we swamp her. If they catch us, all's up!" said the captain.

The boat made good headway but the captain

suddenly shouted: "Hold!" and backed with a great heave that sent the boat's stern under water. At the very same moment they heard the cannon fire.

The ball passed a short way from the boat, but the water they had shipped made the boat begin to sink.

They were able to wade safely ashore, but it meant the loss of all the stores.

While the boat had been moving towards the shore, seven of the pirates had rushed into the wood to cut my friends off from the stockade. Captain Smollett, realising this new danger, urged his companions to hurry, but they were not in time to reach the stockade before the seven mutineers, led by Job Anderson, burst out of the wood, armed with pistols and in full cry. Joyce and Hunter from the block house, and the squire from outside the palisade, opened fire. One of the mutineers fell, the rest turned tail and fled into the wood.

The group went to the fallen mutineer and while they were bending over him, a pistol cracked and the ball hit poor Tom Redruth. The squire and the doctor fired into the wood, then, carried him inside the stockade.

Soon afterwards he died, but there was no chance of burying the poor fellow, because it was necessary to see to the defences and bring in the stores. Captain Smollett arranged guard duties, listed all the stores, then ran up the Union Jack.

This, then, explained the firing and the shots, and the flag waving above the trees. At the sight of it I stopped, but Ben Gunn had an explanation. "Your friends have sheltered in Flint's old stockade," he said.

"Let's go and join them!" I said.

"Jim, you're a good boy," said Ben Gunn. "But I won't follow you. First talk to this squire of yours, and when you want to see Ben Gunn again, you know where to find him. Whoever comes must be carrying something white, and he's to come alone. Let him come between noon and six. And if you meet Silver, not a word about Ben Gunn . . ."

Ben took to his heels and I moved from one hiding place to another. After a long detour I managed to reach the shore. The *Hispaniola* still lay where she had anchored, but the Jolly Roger, the black flag of piracy, fluttered from her mast.

On the beach some men were hacking away with axes at something: our poor little boat. Further away a great fire was blazing surrounded by drunken men.

I crept to the stockade, shouted to my friends inside and quickly climbed in. They listened to my account of what had happened and asked endless questions. Meantime Dr. Livesey had prepared supper, and after the meal we buried poor Tom Redruth, and the captain divided us into watches.

After taking these measures the doctor, the squire and the captain discussed our prospects, which were hardly encouraging.

Our stores were so low that we could not stand up to a long siege. And so, it was decided to reduce the number of pirates as much as possible, and thus force the survivors to surrender or flee. There were now only fifteen of them, two of those wounded. We also had two powerful allies — rum and the climate.

The first of these was already showing its destructive power, for we could hear the mutineers roaring and quarrelling late into the night. As for the second, the doctor said that half of them would be struck down by malaria within ten days at the most.

I was dead tired, and dropped off, waking to the sound of voices. "A white flag," I heard someone say. "Why, it's Silver himself!"

The Pirates Attack the Fortress

Outside the stockade were two men, one holding a white flag and the other — Silver — wearing naval officer's uniform.

"Keep inside," said the captain. "It may be a trick." Then, to the pirates: "Stand, or we fire."

"We're here to make terms," called Silver. "What happened last night won't happen again. You won't get a man creeping up to the camp, because I'll have sentries posted and there'll be no rum given out."

Captain Smollett stared at Silver, though his words must have puzzled him. I imagined (and was later proved right) that Ben Gunn had paid the mutineers a visit during the night while they lay drunk, and had put paid to one of them. So now we had only fourteen enemies to deal with.

"But let's get down to business," Silver went on. "We want that treasure, and we'll have it. You've got Flint's chart, and we need it. If you give us that, we'll give you a choice: either to come on board with us, when the treasure's shipped, and I'll land you safely somewhere; or, I'll leave you half the stores and send the first ship we meet back to pick you up. Those are my terms."

"Is that all?" said the captain. "Now, listen to my terms. If you'll come here one by one, unarmed, I'll clap you in irons and take you to England, where you'll be given a fair trial. If you won't, I'll see you to the devil!"

Silver gave a curse, then started to move away. After a few steps he stopped and shouted: "In an hour, I'll burn you in your old block-house like a barrel of rum! And then you'll know what John Silver's like! The dead will be the lucky ones!"

Captain Smollett ordered us all to our quarters. "My friends," he said, "I've given Silver a broadside, and I did it on purpose. He was so angry he gave away his plans. In an hour he'll attack us. We're outnumbered, but I'm certain we can beat them off. Doctor, you take the door, Hunter, you take the east side; Joyce, you take the west. Mr. Trelawney, you're the best shot, so you and Gray will take this north side, which has five holes. Jim, we'll help to load."

Then he went to see that all was in order.

The hour Silver had allowed us was only just over when Joyce opened fire. The report had barely died away when it was repeated from all round the stockade. When the smoke cleared, the stockade and the woods looked as quiet as before. The enemy had inflicted no losses, and neither had we. Suddenly a group of pirates came roaring out of the wood and rushed towards the stockade, on the side guarded by the squire and Gray, who opened fire at once.

At the same moment, the pirates hidden in the wood opened fire on the other sides of the block-house, and then began to climb over the palisade. Two of them fell under our fire, and a third was wounded, but four came on and were out of the line of fire in a moment.

"We've got them, lads!" shouted one of the pirates, while another snatched Hunter's musket by the muzzle, pulled it through the hole, and pushed it back violently into his face. I saw Hunter fall as a third man appeared and threatened Dr. Livesey with a cutlass.

Our position was now completely reversed: we were open to the enemy. But the block-house was full of smoke, and this was partly what saved us.

"Out, and fight them in the open!" shouted the captain. "Cutlasses!"

We snatched up cutlasses and rushed to the door, where the doctor was overwhelming his attacker. The pirate rolled down the slope, wounded. Captain Smollett continued to shout his orders. "Round the house, lads! We've got to get them out!"

I ran round to the back of the block-house, but found myself face to face with one of the pirates who raised his cutlass to strike me. Gray, who was close behind me, cut him down. A third man had been wounded, and was now lying in a corner.

Other mutineers were trying to scramble in over the palisade. One of them was just going to jump down when he realised that all who had gone before him were out of the fight, except one who was running towards him. He withdrew rapidly and the rest followed. We gathered to count our losses and gains.

Of our friends, Joyce was dead, Hunter was seriously wounded, and the captain had a ball in the shoulder and another wound in the leg.

The mutineers had lost five men, and a sixth man was wounded — eight now remained.

Captain Smollett summed up the situation. "There are four of us left, because I'm out of the fighting, and eight of them. If we could only save Hunter!"

But Hunter died that night.

My Second Escape

Soon after, Dr. Livesey, armed with pistols and a musket, climbed over the palisade and vanished into the wood, making for the interior of the island. It was just after midday.

"He's gone mad, leaving the stockade," remarked Gray. "The pirates may wound him or capture him."

"They won't," I replied. "He's gone to see Ben Gunn, I'm certain."

Later I learnt that my guess had been right. But in the meantime I had the cooking pots to clean, and I suddenly longed to get away. I decided to find Ben Gunn's boat.

I knew I was behaving foolishly, leaving only two sound men to guard the block-house, but I could not stand being cooped up there any longer. So, picking up a few biscuits, pistols and a cutlass, I set off.

By the time I reached the white rock the sun had set and mist was rising. I found a tiny cave, its entrance hidden by a curtain of goatskin. This I pushed aside, and found Ben Gunn's boat.

Now that I had found it, I should have gone back. But I had another plan — to get to the *Hispaniola* under cover of darkness, and cut her adrift while most of the mutineers were on shore.

When I was sure that I could move without being seen, I shouldered the boat, made for the shore, and got to the *Hispaniola*, close to the anchor. I took out my knife and cut through all the hawser's strands except two.

Suddenly I heard the noise of a quarrel on board. Two men, who must have been drunk, were shouting furiously and seemed on the point of coming to blows. One of them was Israel Hands, Flint's one-time gunner; the other, O'Brien, an ordinary sailor.

I slashed through the last strands that held the anchor, and the *Hispaniola* began to turn on her heel, but the mutineers noticed nothing. Finally I heard the noise of things being smashed, and a dull thud; then nothing.

I tried to take my boat towards the shore, but the current forced me out to sea. For what seemed an endless time I fought the tide, and then, overcome with weariness, I lay down and recommended my soul to God, feeling quite certain that in a very short time things were going to end in disaster.

For hours, I stayed there, tossed on the waves, waiting for death. Then I fell asleep.

It was day when I woke. I realised that the current had carried my boat quite near to Treasure Island. I began to paddle towards the shore; but, from behind the promontory not half a mile away, I saw the *Hispaniola*. I realised that nobody was steering. Either the two men were dead drunk, or else had abandoned the schooner, and a new plan suddenly came to me — to get on board and take her to a place of safety.

In spite of the *Hispaniola*'s erratic course, I managed to gain on her, and was circling her, looking for some way of getting aboard, when a particularly powerful wave sent her swooping over me. The bowsprit was over my head, and with a spring I caught the jib-boom and got my foot between the stay and the brace.

I crawled along the bowsprit and tumbled head

first on to the deck. The two mutineers were there, but in no position to stop me.

Israel Hands was crouched in a corner, white-faced. The other man lay stiffened in death.

"I've come to take possession of this ship," I said. "And you'll regard me as your captain!"

"Well, Cap'n Hawkins," said Hands, "you'll want to get ashore now. Without my help, you can't, but if you'll give me food and drink and a handkerchief to tie my wound up, I'll tell you how to sail her."

The *Hispaniola* Recaptured

This seemed to make sense, though I realised Hands was in no way to be trusted. I must pretend to believe him, while keeping a very good eye on him. So I said: "Agreed."

The wind blew just as we wanted it and we soon reached a safe inlet I had chosen. But we had to wait for the tide to flow a good deal further before beaching her. We settled down to wait.

"Cap'n Hawkins," Hands said, "why don't we drink some wine? There's plenty in the cabin."

Clearly it was a trick to get me away from the deck, and I pretended to agree, got up and went towards the cabin; but as soon as I was out of sight I mounted the forecastle ladder, and popped my head out of the companion. From there I saw Hands dragging himself to a coil of rope, taking a blood-stained knife out of it, and hiding it his shirt.

He was now armed, and able to strike me. But I knew he would do nothing until the *Hispaniola* was beached. After that, I must be doubly careful. I stole back, and found a bottle of wine. When I returned Hands was lying where I had left him.

The tide was now in and the ship could be taken to be beached. Hands was the pilot and I carried out his orders promptly. At last, the *Hispaniola* swung round and ran for the low wooded shore. At the same moment I felt a sudden danger and turned; there, a few steps away, stood Hands, dragging his wounded leg and carrying his knife.

I gave a shriek of terror, dropped the rudder and leaped on the deck. Hands followed, trying to pen me in a corner. Out of my pocket I took a pistol but the seawater had dampened the powder and I needed to reprime and reload it. So I climbed the mizzen mast and did not draw breath until I was sitting on the cross-trees. Hands followed, but slowly and painfully, dragging his wounded leg.

I managed to load the pistol before he was near me, and pointed it at him. "One more step, Mr. Hands, and I'll blow your brains out!" I cried.

He stopped and swallowed. "Here," he said "take the knife and throw it away —" and he raised his arm to fling it. But, instead of throwing it overboard, he aimed it at me.

At the very moment in which he was hurling his knife, the *Hispaniola* struck ground and staggered violently. I felt a blow and a sharp pain but managed

to keep hold of the mast. The sudden shock made me press the trigger, and I saw Hands suddenly fling out his arms and plunge head first into the water.

When the *Hispaniola* was beached, she turned on her side and her masts hung far out over the water. The knife, had pinned my shoulder to the mast. My first idea was to pull out the knife, but my nerve failed me, and with a violent shudder I stopped trying to move it. Oddly enough it was the shudder that set me free: it tore away the pinch of skin that was holding me to the mast, and showed me that the wound was neither deep nor dangerous. A few minutes below, and I had bandaged it, then I slipped overboard and made for the shore.

No sooner had I set foot on land than the sun set

and the cold evening breeze began whistling through the tree tops. At last I could make my way back, and I was not returning emptyhanded: the ship was safe and could be easily refloated. I was happy to be going back to my friends. They might scold me for running away, but my capture of the ship would be an answer to that. Besides, I was bringing important news: the number of mutineers was further diminished, since Hands and O'Brien had both ended their wretched lives.

At last I reached the stockade. Part of the palisade was steeped in moonlight, while the rest of it, and the block-house, were in darkness. An enormous fire, now a heap of embers, spread a reddish glow. I stopped in amazement: who had disobeyed Captain Smollett's orders not to light large fires?

Well, there must be some reason for it, I supposed. Without making the slightest sound I reached the block-house, thinking that my friends kept a very poor watch.

At the door I stopped: inside it was dark, but I heard a quiet, reassuring sound of snoring.

Noiselessly I crept in.

In the darkness I tripped over something soft: the leg of a sleeper who muttered and turned over without waking. But a shrill voice suddenly shouted: "Pieces of eight! Pieces of eight! Pieces of eight!"

It was Silver's parrot!

A sudden uproar greeted the parrot's cry, with Silver's voice roaring above the rest: "Who goes?"

I shook myself and tried to run, but someone seized my arms.

"Bring a torch, Dick," said Silver, and its glare lit me and the man who had caught me.

Prisoner of the Pirates

They all stood round, staring at me without a word.

Silver at last broke the silence. "Jim, this is a fine surprise. Right from the start I hoped you'd join us, and now you've got to. You can't go back to your friends, because they're too angry with you; you'll have to join us."

"If I'm to choose," I said, "I must know where my friends have gone and why you're here. I can only make a choice if you tell me plainly."

"Perfectly fair," said Silver. "Yesterday morning the doctor came to us carrying a white flag and said: 'Silver, the ship's disappeared. Let's bargain.' So we did, and now we're here in Flint's old block-house and I don't know where they are. You weren't included in the agreement, mind."

"I'm not such a fool as not to know what I can hope for from you," I replied. "But I don't care. I've got something to tell you, though. You're in a bad way: you've lost the ship, the treasure, and most of your men. In fact, you're done for. And if you want to know who brought you to it, I'll tell you. I did! I was in the apple barrel the night you talked to some of the men. I heard all your plans and told what I'd heard. It was I who cut the ship's cable, I who killed the men on board and I who landed her safely. If anyone here has a choice to make, it's you, not me. You can kill me or spare me. But if you spare me, when you're on trial for piracy I'll save you if I can."

"Kill him!" roared the mutineers. "Kill the boy!"

"Stop!" ordered Silver, as one of the pirates came at me. "I'll decide what to do with the boy. I like him. He's more a man than any pair of rats in this house!"

There was a long pause after this. I stood straight up against the wall, my heart thumping. Silver leant back against the wall, his arms crossed, calm; yet his eyes kept wandering furtively. His followers had come together at the far end of the block-house, and we could hear the low hiss of their whispered talk.

"You seem to have a lot to say," remarked Silver. "Pipe up and let me hear it."

"This crew's dissatisfied," answered one of the men. "We claim our right to step outside for a council."

One by one the men left the block-house.

When they had all gone, Silver spoke in a whisper. "Jim, you're not far from death. They want to throw me off because I stood up for you. I know all's lost and I said to myself: 'You can save Jim, and he'll save you.' Now, be very careful. I won't ask you any more questions about the ship and where you've got her. But there's one thing I want to ask you: why d'you think the doctor gave me Flint's chart?"

I looked so astonished that Silver gave up asking

more questions. "Well, never mind. He did, though. And for his own good reasons. But . . ."

The door opened. The mutineers pushed one of their number forward; he passed something to Silver.

"Silver, the crew's decided to give you the black spot," said a tall man. "Now, turn over the paper, and see what's written. That's your duty."

"I see you've gone by the rules and deposed me. The rules say you've got to tell me your grievances and I'm to reply. Till then, I'm still captain!"

"We'll stick to the rules, then," said the tall man. "These are our grievances: first, you've made a hash of the cruise; second, you let the enemy out of the trap, and last, you won't settle the boy. What do you say to that?"

"Plenty," said Silver, perfectly calm. "First of all, if you'd followed my plan we'd all be safe and sound on the *Hispaniola*, and the treasure with us. Who forced my hand the day we landed on the island? Next, you accuse me of bargaining with the enemy. But who kept complaining of the fever, who was starving to death? I've got it all fixed up — food to eat and even a doctor to come every day. And as for the boy — why, he's our hostage, our last chance. But here's the real reason why I bargained!"

He flung down Flint's chart of the island.

If I was surprised, the mutineers were astounded. They leapt on the chart, snatching it from one another and remarking on everything about it.

"Yes, it's Flint's chart!" said one man. "I recognise his writing."

"But how shall we carry the treasure to the ship?" said another.

"That's up to you," said Silver. "You'll have to see to that, because I'm having nothing more to do with a good-for-nothing lot like you!"

"No, no," they all shouted. "Barbecue for ever! Barbecue for captain!"

"So that's it, is it?" said Silver, triumphantly. "Come on, lads, let's get to sleep, and tomorrow morning no one'll remember what you did. I'm not vindictive, as you know!"

The mutineers all drank to their new friendship, then lay down to sleep.

It was some time before I could sleep, for what was occupying my mind was Silver's remarkable game — keeping the pirates together on the one hand, and at the same time doing all he could to bargain with us and save his own life.

Treasure-hunting with Silver

I was woken by a voice calling from the wood. It was Dr. Livesey.

"We've got a surprise for you, doctor. A new boarder . . ." said Silver.

"Not Jim?" said the doctor, and Silver confirmed that it was. "Well, well! But duty first and pleasure afterwards. Let's see these patients of yours."

He came into the block-house, and set to.

"Now, I'd like a word with that boy," he said when he had seen to them.

"If Jim will give me his word not to escape," said Silver.

I gave him my word, and Silver took me over to the palisade. Dr. Livesey stood on the other side and as soon as we were out of earshot of the men, who were watching us, Silver said: "Jim will tell you I saved his life and that they tried to depose me for it. But I managed to make them change their minds and keep the boy as hostage. You're an honest man, sir, and you won't forget that, will you?" And, without waiting for a reply, he moved away.

Briefly I described my adventures, and when I had finished the doctor murmured:

"It's fate: every step we take you save our lives. Finding Ben Gunn, too, was the best thing you could have done, but . . . I forgot! Silver, come here. I've a piece of advice!" When Silver came over, he said, "Don't be in a hurry looking for the treasure."

"It's by looking that I can save my life and Jim's."

"Well, I suggest you keep a close watch while you're searching. I can't say more, but if we ever get out of this I'll do what I can to save you." And, with a handshake for me, Dr. Livesey was gone.

"Jim," said Silver when we were alone, "we must start looking for the treasure, but stick close to me, so that we can save ourselves if things go wrong."

Straight after breakfast we set off on the treasure

hunt. Silver told the men that as soon as they found the gold, they could do what they liked with me. As he said this he winked at me, but even today I feel sure that if things had gone the way Silver planned, he would not have hesitated to hand me over.

Thanks to Flint's chart, we found the Spyglass shown on the chart. As we were climbing the hill, we heard a hoarse voice raised in song — a song we all knew well: "Fifteen men on a dead man's chest — Yo-ho-ho, and a bottle of rum!"

The effect this produced on the pirates was indescribable: they all looked as if they had seen a ghost.

"It's Flint's ghost!" shrieked one of the mutineers.

Silver had turned pale, but I saw him overcome his fear and raise his fist in the direction of the mysterious voice.

"Flint didn't scare me when he was alive," he cried. "D'you think he's going to scare me now he's dead? The devil himself won't stop me! There's seven hundred thousand pounds waiting for us!"

The voice was now silent and the mutineers almost ran the last part of the journey, Silver hobbling beside me. I saw that now that we were near the treasure he had forgotten not only what he had said to Dr. Livesey, but the doctor's advice to him. All he now had in mind was to get hold of the gold, seize the ship, and kill any honest men left on the island.

At last we saw a tall tree, quite clearly the one marked on Flint's chart. At the sight of it the men started running towards it, but after a moment they stopped dead, with a low cry. Before them lay a great hole, not very recently dug, in the bottom of which lay the remains of a wooden chest: the treasure had been taken away.

"So this is your seven hundred thousand pounds! This is what your bargaining's brought us to!" shouted one of the men. "Mates, there's only two of them. An old cripple and a young cub. Kill . . ."

He never finished the sentence. Three musket shots flashed from the wood and he and another man tumbled into the hole. The other three turned and ran. At the same moment Dr. Livesey, Gray and Ben Gunn, came out of the wood.

"Ben Gunn," murmured Silver. "Now I see it all."

Ben Gunn, who had mimicked Flint's voice to scare the mutineers, had found the treasure, and after digging it up had taken it to the cave where he lived. Dr. Livesey had got the secret during his talk with Ben Gunn on the day I escaped, then he had given Silver Flint's map in exchange for getting out of the stockade. My friends had withdrawn to Ben Gunn's cave, and that morning, knowing that I was to be involved in the mutineers' terrible disappointment, they had decided to lie in wait and free me.

The squire had stayed in the cave with Captain Smollett, and Ben Gunn had run ahead to slow the pirates down by frightening them. Everything had gone according to plan, but we now had to make sure that the three men still at large could do nothing to harm us. We went to the beach, launched a boat, and set off to find the *Hispaniola*.

She was where I had left her. Another anchor was dropped, then we returned to Ben Gunn's cave.

In the days that followed we loaded the treasure on to the *Hispaniola* and saw no sign of the surviving mutineers. We left food and powder, and had only just left when the three men came out of the wood, flung themselves on their knees and held their hands out beseechingly. It seemed terrible to leave them but we could not risk another mutiny.

Having no crew, we sailed for the nearest port. We went ashore to look for men to sail with us, and when we returned Silver had gone, with one of the sacks of coin. I think we were glad to be rid of him.

We reached Bristol just in time to stop the ship sailing to rescue us. Of those that had sailed, only five had returned. The survivors got their share, and spent it wisely or foolishly, according to their nature.

Captain Smollett retired from the sea. Gray decided to study, and became mate and part-owner of a fine ship. Ben Gunn spent his share in three weeks, and is now porter in a lodge, with moderate success. Of Silver we heard no more, but I am sure he is living prosperously somewhere. Nor have we ever heard of the mutineers we left on the island, but of one thing I am quite certain: I would never go back there. In my dreams I often leap out of bed in terror of the sound of Silver's parrot screaming in my ears: "Pieces of eight! Pieces of eight!"